GROWL!

D0263691

READZ🦉NE
ReadZone Books Limited

First published in this edition 2015

© in this edition ReadZone Books Limited 2015
© in text Vivian French 2007
© in illustrations Tim Archbold 2007

Vivian French has asserted her right under the Copyright Designs
and Patents Act 1988 to be identified as the author of this work.

Tim Archbold has asserted his right under the Copyright Designs
and Patents Act 1988 to be identified as the illustrator of this work.

Every attempt has been made by the Publisher to secure appropriate
permissions for material reproduced in this book. If there has been any
oversight we will be happy to rectify the situation in future editions or
reprints. Written submissions should be made to the Publisher.

British Library Cataloguing in Publication Data (CIP) is available
for this title.

Printed in Malta by Melita Press.

All rights reserved. No part of this publication may be reproduced,
stored in a retrieval system or transmitted, in any form or by any
means, electronic, mechanical, photocopying, recording or otherwise,
without the prior permission of ReadZone Books Limited.

ISBN 978 1 78322 412 8

Visit our website: www.readzonebooks.com

GROWL!

Vivian French
and Tim Archbold

On the edge of the woods was a little
blue house. Inside the house lived
Mr and Mrs Wolf, Baby Wolf, and
a GREAT BIG MONSTER who was
very VERY fierce. Even at breakfast.

"Grrrr!" growled Wally the great big monster. "Grrr! Grrr! Grrr!"

"Wally," said his mother, "PLEASE stop growling. You're scaring your little sister."

Grrr!

Grrr!

"GRRR!" said Wally, even louder.

Wally's mother frowned. "Wally," she said, "if you don't stop growling THIS MINUTE you will NOT be allowed to go fishing."

Grrr!

Wally stopped growling and ate his breakfast. After he'd finished he went to find his fishing rod.

"Grrr!" he growled as he came to say goodbye.

Mrs Wolf sighed. "Have a lovely time, Wally dear," she said. "And be very careful."

"GRRRRRRR!" growled Wally, and he stamped off and away along the path.

On the other side of the woods
was a little red house.

Inside the house lived Mr and Mrs Bear, Baby Bear and a TERRIBLE SCARY CREATURE who was very VERY frightening. Even at breakfast.

"Grrr!" growled Bobbie. "Grrr! Grrr! Grrr!"

"Bobbie," said her dad, "You've been growling for days and DAYS and I'm tired of it.

Please stop RIGHT NOW, or you can't go fishing."

Grrr!

Bobbie stopped growling and gobbled her breakfast. Then she jumped down from the table and went to find her fishing rod.

"Bobbie!" her dad called after her. "Be careful! The pond is very deep!"

"GRRRRRRR!" growled Bobbie as she skipped down the path.

Wally stamped towards the pond.
"I'm the biggest monster in the whole
wide world," he said to himself. "And I
can scare ANYTHING!'

On the other side of the woods Bobbie was skipping towards the pond.

"I'm the scariest creature in the whole wide world," she said to herself. "And I can scare ANYTHING!"

Wally and Bobbie arrived at the
pond together.
    Wally looked at Bobbie.

Bobbie looked at Wally.

"Grrr!" said Wally.
Bobbie didn't move.

Grrr!

"Grrr!" said Bobbie.
Wally didn't run away.

Grrr!

Grrr!

"GRRR!" growled Wally.
"GRRR!" growled Bobbie.

Grrr!

"GRRR!" growled Wally.
"GRRR!" growled Bobbie.

They growled and they growled
and they GROWLED until they
were both out of breath…

...and then they looked at each other ... and neither of them moved and the wood was VERY quiet until –

RIBBIT!

A frog jumped out of the pond.
"AAAAAAGH!" yelled Wally.
"OOOOOOH!" shrieked Bobbie.

And they both ran
home just as fast as they
could go.

"Are you still a big fierce monster?"
Wally's Mum asked.

"No," said Wally. "I'm a little wolf
and I want a hug."

"Are you still a terrible scary creature?" Asked Bobbie's Dad.

"No," said Bobbie. "I'm a little bear and I want a cuddle."

"Grrr," said Bobbie's little brother.
"Grrr. Grrr. GRR!"

Grrr!

"Grrr," said Wally's little sister. "Grrr! Grr! GRR!"

Grrr!

Did you enjoy this book?

Look out for more *Magpies* titles –
fun stories in 150 words

The Clumsy Cow by Julia Moffat and Lisa Williams
ISBN 978 1 78322 157 8

The Disappearing Cheese by Paul Harrison and Ruth Rivers
ISBN 978 1 78322 470 8

Flying South by Alan Durant and Kath Lucas
ISBN 978 1 78322 410 4

Fred and Finn by Madeline Goodey and Mike Gordon
ISBN 978 1 78322 411 1

Growl! by Vivian French and Tim Archbold
ISBN 978 1 78322 412 8

I Wish I Was an Alien by Vivian French and Lisa Williams
ISBN 978 1 78322 413 5

Lovely, Lovely Pirate Gold by Scoular Anderson
ISBN 978 1 78322 206 3

Pet to School Day by Hilary Robinson and Tim Archbold
ISBN 978 1 78322 471 5

Tall Tilly by Jillian Powell and Tim Archbold
ISBN 978 1 78322 414 2

Terry the Flying Turtle by Anna Wilson and Mike Gordon
ISBN 978 1 78322 415 9

Too Small by Kay Woodward and Deborah van de Leijgraaf
ISBN 978 1 78322 156 1

Turn Off the Telly by Charlie Gardner and Barbara Nascimbeni
ISBN 978 1 78322 158 5